The
Railway
Rabbits

Mellow and the Great River Rescue

The
Railway
Rabbits

Mellow and the Great River Rescue

Orion
Children's Books

First published in Great Britain in 2011
by Orion Children's Books
a division of the Orion Publishing Group Ltd
Orion House
5 Upper St Martin's Lane
London WC2H 9EA
An Hachette UK Company

1 3 5 7 9 10 8 6 4 2

ISBN 978 1 4440 0161 7

www.orionbooks.co.uk

For Anna Currey, whose illustrations
complement my stories beautifully. Lucky
rabbits. Lucky me!

G.A.

The Ripple River Valley

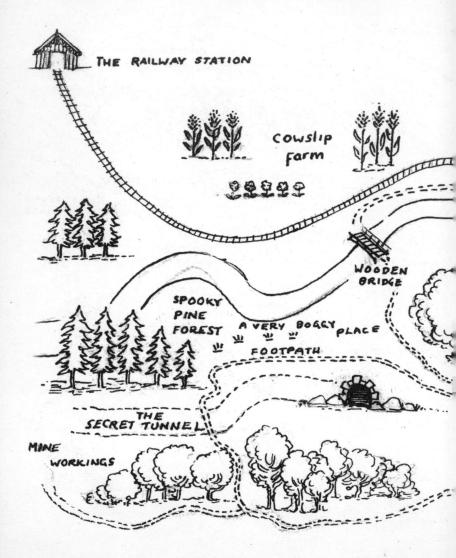

THE RAILWAY STATION

COWSLIP FARM

WOODEN BRIDGE

SPOOKY PINE FOREST

A VERY BOGGY PLACE

FOOTPATH

THE SECRET TUNNEL

MINE WORKINGS

Weather Warnings
1

Early one summer's morning, Mellow
Longears was getting ready to leave
the burrow. She was taking Bramble,
Bracken, Berry, Fern and Wisher to
see their elders, Eyebright and Willow
Silvercoat. It was the first time the young
rabbits had visited Mellow's parents and
they were all very excited.

"You must eat something before we go," said Mellow. "It's quite a hop along the riverbank."

"Whaar do our eldersh liff?" asked Berry. His words sounded funny because his mouth was full of dandelion leaves.

"Please don't talk while you're eating, Berry," said Mellow. "Eldermarr and Elderparr Silvercoat live at Burrow Bank."

"Where's that?" said Bracken.

"Downriver," said Mellow. "Burrow Bank is close to the Red Dragon's tracks."

"Ooo!" said Fern. "I hope we don't get caught by the monster!"

"So do I," said Wisher.

"He won't catch me!" said Bramble. "I always know when the Dragon is about. He makes such a noise!"

"You'll be safe as long as you keep out of his way," said Mellow. "Remember what I always say: sensible rabbits have careful habits!"

Barley Longears had been listening to their conversation and he was looking more and more worried. He paced up and down, tugging his ear.

"I wish I was coming with you," he said. "But I must guard our burrow. I hope you'll be all right. Maybe I *should* come? Oh, buttercups! I don't know what to do. You will be careful, won't you?"

"Of course," said Mellow. "Don't worry, Barley. We won't be gone for long."

"Be good," Barley told his five young rabbits. "Stay with Marr. Don't go running off on your own! Keep your eyes open for Burdock and owls and foxes . . ."

"Parr!" said Bramble, Bracken, Berry, Fern and Wisher. "We KNOW!"

"Parr is right," Mellow told them. Then to Barley she said: "I'm *quite* capable of looking after our children for one day, Barley Longears!"

"True," he said. "But it won't stop me worrying my whiskers off!"

Mellow kissed his nose, and off they went.

Mellow led Bramble, Bracken, Berry, Fern
and Wisher down to the river and over the
little wooden bridge. Halfway across they
stopped to look down at their reflections
in the water. This In-Not-Such-A-Hurry
River was flowing gently along as if it had
all the time in the world. Fern sang a little
song and the others joined in.

"The River Ripple is its name,
Long may it gently flow.
So let us thank the hare who came
And danced so long ago."

"The river was made from teardrops, wasn't it, Marr?" said Wisher. She remembered a story they'd been told about a dancing hare and a sad princess.

"That's right," said Mellow. "The princess cried so much *'her tears like raindrops fell . . .'*"

A sudden movement below caught everyone's attention. It was Violet Vole, swimming out from under the bridge.

"Hello," said Violet. "I thought I heard voices.

Something about rain. It doesn't look like rain. A few clouds maybe, but a good day to be out and about, wouldn't you say? Well, I suppose you would because you *are* out and about, aren't you? Silly me! Where are you going? Somewhere nice?"

"We're visiting my parents down at Burrow Bank," said Mellow.

"A day out with the family," said Violet. "How lovely! Now, I must be off. I have food to find and mouths to feed. Busy, busy me. Goodbye!"

Violet swam away and the rabbits
continued over the bridge. On the other
side, Mellow took them along a path
that ran by the river. The banks
were full of pretty yellow,
blue and pink wildflowers
and she pointed them out as
they hopped along:

"Buttercup. Clover. Daisy.
Harebell . . ."

Berry was soon bored.

"Look at me," he said, flipping a
somersault. He lost his balance, rolled
down a slope and landed in a patch
of thistles.

"Ow, ow, ow!" he cried.

"Serves you right," said Mellow,
hiding a smile.

The others helped to pull him up. It was then Mellow noticed someone was missing.

"Where's Bramble?" she said.

"He ran ahead," said Bracken. "When we stopped to help Berry."

"Oh no!" said Fern. "What if Burdock sees him?"

"Or a fox," said Wisher.

"He can't have gone far," said Mellow, trying to keep calm. "Come on. Let's go after him."

They raced along the path. Soon, to Mellow's relief, they saw him. He was sitting by a tree – ears pricked, nose sniffing.

"What did Parr tell you? We *must* keep together!" Mellow said crossly.

Bramble defended himself.

"I was keeping a look-out for danger, Marr," he said. "If I'd spotted Burdock, I'd have warned you." He thumped his hind-foot on the path three times – *thump, thump, thump!* It was the warning signal Barley had taught all the young rabbits.

Mellow sighed. She knew how Bramble liked to take charge.

"Thank you," she said. "But you gave me a fright!"

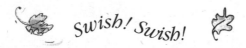

Swish! Swish!

A rustle of leaves above made them all look up.

A grey-coated animal with a bushy tail
was jumping through the branches.

It was Sylvia Squirrel. She climbed
down the tree trunk to join them.

"Hello," said Sylvia. "I couldn't help
overhearing. Children can be such a
worry, can't they? You have to keep your
eye on them *all* the time. One blink and
they're away . . ."

"Bramble was trying to protect us," said Mellow.

"How brave!" said Sylvia. She beamed round at the others. "Going far?"

"We're visiting our elders," said Fern.

"At Burrow Bank," said Berry.

"I hope you won't get caught in the rain," said Sylvia.

"Rain?" said Mellow.

Sylvia nodded.

"My tail has been twitching all morning," she said. "It's a sure sign."

Wisher, who had been half-listening, half-daydreaming, tugged Mellow's paw.

"Marr, my ears are tingling," she said. "I can hear a voice inside my head . . ."

Summer raindrops from the sky, Will bring trouble, by and by!

"There you are!" said Sylvia. "What did I say? My tail is always right."

"Well," said Mellow. "We must hurry. Thank you, Sylvia. Goodbye."

Mellow, Bramble, Bracken, Berry, Fern and Wisher left Sylvia gazing up at the sky. As they came to a bend in the river, the rabbits saw Daisy Duck. She was out on the water with her new ducklings. Six tiny balls of feathers were paddling round in circles!

"Hello!" quacked Daisy. "I'm teaching my babies to swim. This is their first day out."

"Good luck!" cried Mellow.

Wisher watched the baby ducklings swirling round and round, and felt her ears tingle. Again she heard the warning voice inside her head:

Summer raindrops from the sky,
Will bring trouble, by and by!

Wondering what it could mean, Wisher hurried after the others.

The Silvercoats of Burrow Bank
2

Plip, plap, plop!

The first few raindrops fell as the rabbits were arriving at Burrow Bank. Down they splashed, one by one.

"My nose!" said Berry.

"My eye!" said Fern.

"My ears!" said Wisher.

"My tail!" said Bracken.

"My head!" said Bramble.

Mellow shook drops from her paw. "Sylvia was right," she said.

The summer shower quickly turned into a downpour and in no time the rabbits were very wet. Luckily, just ahead they could see a high bank full of rabbit holes. Bramble, Bracken, Berry, Fern and Wisher had never seen so many burrows in one place.

"Which one belongs to Elderparr and Eldermarr?" shouted Bramble above the noisy rain.

"I'm not sure," cried Mellow. "I haven't been here for a while. But I know it's near the top . . ." Then she spotted two rabbits outside a burrow. "There they are!"

They all raced up the steep bank.

"Marr! Parr!" cried Mellow, hugging them.

"Oh, my whiskers!" said Elderparr Eyebright. "It's raining rabbits." He was holding a large dock leaf, trying to shelter everyone. "Quickly. Hop inside."

"Let's get you dry or you'll catch the sneezes," said Eldermarr Willow, hurrying them down a narrow passage.

On the way, they passed a tunnel branching off to the left. The sound of voices talking and laughing drifted along the walls.

"Who lives down there?" asked Mellow.

"Our neighbours," said Willow. "Lop and Lilly Greyback."

"Lop and Lilly!" cried Mellow, surprised. "We used to play together."

"Well," said Willow. "Lilly is a mother now, like you. The Greybacks have identical twins, Tansy and Teasel. They're a lively pair, those two, always up to mischief."

Berry pricked his ears. Tansy and Teasel sounded fun!

After a few more twists and turns, Willow brought them into a small cave.

"Here we are," she said.  "Now you can dry your coats!"

The rabbits shook water from their fur. Elderparr Eyebright looked at Bramble, Bracken, Berry, Fern and Wisher in turn.

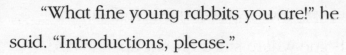

"What fine young rabbits you are!" he said. "Introductions, please."

They hopped up and told him their names.

"I'm Bramble."

"I'm Bracken."

"I'm Berry."

"I'm Fern."

"And I'm Wisher."

Wisher thought Eyebright looked very handsome. He had a thick, silvery coat and his eyes twinkled like stars. Eldermarr Willow had smooth, grey-brown fur and big soft eyes – just like Marr's.

"Welcome to Burrow Bank!" said Eyebright. "Have a look around."

Mellow enjoyed being back in the home where she'd grown up. She had lived here with her two brothers and three sisters. It was a cosy burrow with nooks and hollows for sleeping and storing food. Twisted tree roots entwined themselves in the roof and walls, and on the floor there was a carpet of dried flowers.

"Mmm! Honeysuckle and lavender," said Mellow to Eldermarr Willow. "You taught me the names of plants."

"Marr showed us some on the way here," said Fern.

"I'm glad to hear it," said Willow. "You must try to remember them."

Just then, a drop of rain plopped on the floor.

Splat!

Eyebright looked up. A trickle of water was coming through a tiny hole in the roof. It was raining so heavily, they could hear it beating down above their heads.

"Fish swim. Frogs hop. I'll eat my tail if this rain doesn't stop!" he cried, jumping up and down.

Bramble, Bracken, Berry, Fern and Wisher laughed.

"I *think* I know where I get my sayings from," said Mellow with a smile. "I take after you, Parr!"

The young rabbits knew just what she meant.

"Silly rabbits have careless habits!" they sang.

"Yes," said Mellow. "That's one of my favourites."

"And a good one too!" said Eyebright.

It rained and rained. There was nothing to do but wait for it to stop. The young rabbits soon grew restless listening to the grown-ups chatter!

"I'm bored," said Bramble. "I want to explore."

"Me too," said Bracken and Fern.

"I can't wait to go up-burrow," said Wisher.

"We might see Tansy and Teasel," said Berry.

"WHO?" said the others.

"They're twins," said Berry. "They live next-burrow. I heard Eldermarr Willow telling Marr. She said they get up to mischief!"

"Hm? Interesting," said Bramble.

"Fun," said Bracken.

"New friends," said Fern.

Then Wisher's ears tingled the way
they'd done earlier.

Summer raindrops from the sky,
Will bring trouble, by and by!

Eldermarr Willow noticed the puzzled
look on Wisher's face.

"What is it?" she asked gently.

"I hear voices sometimes . . ." said
Wisher.

"Her ears go funny," said Bramble.

"Wisher knows things before they happen," said Bracken.

"She's usually right," said Berry.

"Always," said Fern firmly. "Wisher told us the rain would bring trouble. Something terrible is going to happen, I know it. What if the rain doesn't stop? It might go on for EVER. We'll have to swim home and . . ."

Bramble, Bracken and Berry rolled their eyes. They were used to Fern making a fuss.

"I'm sure that won't be necessary, Fern," said Mellow.

Eldermarr Willow turned to Wisher.

"You have special powers," she said. "A gift passed to you from your great-great-eldermarr, Meadow Silvercoat."

Wisher nodded. "Eldermarr Primrose told me once," she said.

"Ah, yes," said Willow. "Primrose Longears of Deep Burrow. Your parr's marr."

Wisher was only half-listening. She was still thinking about Meadow Silvercoat.

"I wish I'd known her," she said. "Maybe she could have explained how my powers work."

Then Elderparr Eyebright joined in.

"Meadow Silvercoat was a wonderful rabbit!" he said. "It's thanks to her that we Silvercoats are here today.

"Gather round, everyone. I shall tell you a story that has been passed from rabbit to rabbit for as long as anyone can remember . . ."

"Many moons ago," began Eyebright, "Meadow Silvercoat lived on a farm."

"Like Fairweather's Farm Park?" said Bramble. "I rescued a chick there once."

"Er, no," said Eyebright. "Fairweather's is a good farm. The animals are well cared for. At the place I'm talking about rabbits were locked up together in a great, big cage. Can you imagine such a thing?"

Bracken thought of Nigel, a rabbit he'd met once. Nigel had told him he loved living in his hutch. But Bracken had a feeling Elderparr Eyebright was talking about something quite different.

"People-folk made clothes from the rabbits' fine, silvery fur," said Eyebright. "Believe it or not, they wore hats, gloves and coats made from fur like mine. Some of them looked more like rabbits than rabbits! But I was telling you about Meadow Silvercoat. She was born and lived in a cage with lots of other rabbits. Her mother had once lived in a burrow, but she'd been caught and brought to the farm. She told Meadow about the beautiful world outside. The wonderful smell of fresh green grass. How good it felt to hop in the fields. The farmer kept so many rabbits in one place, there was barely enough room to turn round. And they were always hungry. He gave everyone just enough food and water to grow into big rabbits, then . . ."

He paused, choosing his next words carefully.

"Well, rabbits were removed from the cage and never seen again. One day, when Meadow was about your age, young Longears, her parents were taken. Poor Meadow cried and cried. Then, that same night, a strange thing happened. As she tried to settle down to sleep, she felt her ears tingle and she heard a strange voice:

'I whisper a song like the wind in your ear.
Meadow beware. Meadow, take care!
Escape tonight! Leave this farm.
Tomorrow brings only sorrow and harm!'

Meadow woke her friends and told them they were in great danger. They *had* to escape that night! She worked out a plan. The rabbits would gnaw through the cage door with their sharp teeth. It took a while, but at last they made a hole large enough for even the biggest rabbit to squeeze through. By the light of a full moon, they ran and kept on running – far away from that dreadful place.

Thanks to Meadow's warning, all the rabbits were saved. The Silvercoats made homes for themselves and their families along this very river valley. In time, Meadow grew up and met Barleycorn Longears – your great-great-elderparr. And they lived happily at Deep Burrow till the end of their days."

"I'd hate to be locked up!" said Bramble.

"I'm glad they got away," said Fern.

Wisher was thinking about the voice Meadow had heard inside her head.

"I wonder if it's the same one that speaks to me," she said.

Just then, Eyebright twitched his ears.

"Listen!" he said.

The burrow was silent.

"I can't hear anything," said Mellow.

"Exactly!" said Eyebright. "It's stopped raining. We can all go up-burrow!"

Mellow
Meets Old
Friends
3

Burrow Bank was alive with rabbits!
The sun had brought everyone out into
its warmth. Mellow caught sight of Lilly
Greyback. She hadn't seen Lilly for a long
time, but she recognised her at once.

"I'd know those floppy ears anywhere!"
said Mellow, hopping over to greet her
old friend.

"Mellow Longears!" cried Lilly. "What
are you doing here?" She gave Mellow
a hug. "I must fetch my husband, Lop.

You remember Lop? He's around here somewhere. We have twins, Tansy and Teasel. Where are they? They're always running off . . ."

Mellow laughed.

"All in good time, Lilly," she said. "I'm visiting my parents, Eyebright and Willow. I have three bucks and two does of my own. They're here now. Oh, we have *so* much to talk about!"

Bramble, Bracken, Berry, Fern and Wisher raced down the steep bank. The grass was wet and slippery after the rain. Berry slid down a slope and fell in a puddle at the bottom.

"Ugh!" he cried.

The others fell about laughing. Then they all jumped in and out of puddles – *sploosh, splosh, splash!* – and got very muddy!

The young rabbits were having so much fun they didn't notice the Red Dragon's tracks only a few hops away.

Willow and Eyebright ran towards them, panting and out of breath.

"Stay clear!" cried Willow.

"The Red Dragon's coming!" shouted Eyebright.

Whooo-Wheeep!

They heard the wail of a whistle. The massive red beast came thundering down the line, spitting sparks and belching smoke.

Bramble, Bracken, Berry, Fern and Wisher felt the ground shake beneath their paws as it clattered by, blasting them with its hot, steamy breath. It was pulling three carriages full of people-folk who waved at the rabbits as they passed. Then it was gone, rattling down the line –

Clickerty-clack. Clickerty-click!

"The Dragon huffs and puffs a lot," said Eyebright, "but he means us no harm if we stay out of his way."

Mellow rushed over.

"Is everyone all right?" she asked anxiously.

Five grubby faces looked up and nodded.

"Look at you," said Mellow. "Covered in mud!"

"We were only playing . . ." said Berry.

"Hm!" said Mellow. "You were too near the tracks! I nearly got caught by the Dragon once. I'll never forget it."

Willow and Eyebright remembered.

"You were just a baby," said Willow.

"You gave us quite a scare!" said Eyebright.

"Tell us what happened, Marr!" shouted the young rabbits.

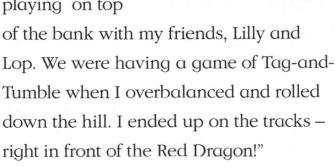

"Well," said Mellow. "I was playing on top of the bank with my friends, Lilly and Lop. We were having a game of Tag-and-Tumble when I overbalanced and rolled down the hill. I ended up on the tracks – right in front of the Red Dragon!"

"Oooo!" said the five young Longears.

"I was SO afraid," said Mellow. "I shook from head to tail."

"We heard a terrible screeching noise," said Eldermarr Willow.

"The Dragon stopped just in time," said Elderparr Eyebright.

"I was very lucky," said Mellow. "I knew, from that day, never to play near his tracks."

A few minutes later, Lilly brought Lop over to Mellow and her parents. The young rabbits groaned.

"Grown-ups love talking!" said Bramble.

"Boring!" said Bracken.

"They'll be there for ages," said Berry.

"For EVER!" said Fern.

"Marr," said Wisher. "Can we play?"

"As long as you stay where I can see you," said Mellow.

"We promise!" said Bramble, Bracken, Berry, Fern and Wisher, as they hopped away to explore.

New Friends and a Dare
4

"Wheeeeee!" shouted Tansy Greyback, sliding sideways down a muddy bank.

"Watch out," cried Teasel Greyback. "Here I come!" He whizzed after her.

The twins landed in a jumbled heap at the bottom. They looked up to see five rabbits they'd never seen before.

"Who are you?" they said.

Bramble, Bracken, Berry, Fern and Wisher introduced themselves.

The two muddy Greybacks stood up and gave cheeky grins.

"I'm Tansy," said Tansy. "And this is my brother, Teasel."

"Hi!" said Teasel.

"We're twins!" they said together.

"We look exactly the same," said Tansy. "Except Teasel's ears flop. Mine don't. They're perfectly straight."

"I like my floppy ears," said Teasel proudly. "They're like Marr's. All the best rabbits have floppy ears!"

The two were very dirty, so it was difficult for the young Longears to tell what Tansy and Teasel looked like. But they could see patches of grey fur, and their paws and tummies were white – or would be when they were clean!

"We're visiting our elders," said Bramble. "Eyebright and Willow Silvercoat."

"They live next-burrow to us!" said Tansy.

"We know," said Berry. "We heard you!"

"I bet that was my sister," said Teasel. "She never stops talking!"

"That's because I'm very clever and have lots of interesting things to say," said Tansy.

Bramble, Bracken, Berry, Fern and
Wisher liked their new friends at once.

"Come and play," said Teasel.

"We'll show you around," said Tansy.

"I can't wait," said Bramble.

The seven young rabbits hurried down to
the River Ripple. Only Wisher noticed how
it had changed since the heavy rainfall.
The water was higher up its banks and,
in places, she could see it had flooded.
Where there had
been grass earlier,
there was now
water.

The river swirled and rushed along faster than Wisher had ever seen before. She thought the river must be in a very bad mood! The tips of her ears tingled.

She joined the others, but now didn't seem the right time to tell everyone how she felt. They were all excited. Tansy and Teasel pointed to a little island in the middle of the river.

"That's our secret place," said Tansy. "We call it River Island!"

"No one's allowed, except us," said Teasel. "Unless they're . . . off-ish-ully invited."

"He means officially," said Tansy. "You know. Done properly." She cleared her throat. "We, Tansy and Teasel Greyback, invite you, Bramble, Bracken, Berry, Fern and Wisher Longears, to River Island! There. It's official. You're invited!"

"Thanks," said Bramble. "Let's go!"

Bracken looked worried. There was a lot of water between themselves and the island.

"Er, how do we get there?" he asked.

"Swim?" said Berry, half-joking.

"Jump?" said Fern nervously.

"How?" said Wisher.

"We hop across," said Teasel.

"On stepping-stones!" said Tansy.

Fern and Wisher looked at each other and then at the

rocks jutting out of the river. The water was rushing over them.

"It's dangerous!" said Fern.

"And slippery," said Wisher.

Bramble hopped forward. He wanted to prove how brave he was to their new friends.

"Watch me," he said. "I'll go first."

Bracken gulped.

"Um. I'll b-b-be right behind you," he said nervously.

Wisher could see he was frightened.

"Wait," she said. "The river looks *very* angry!"

"Maybe Wisher's right," said Berry. "Her voices warned us about trouble, remember?"

"What voices?" said Tansy.

"What trouble?" said Teasel.

"It's my ears," said Wisher. "I can't explain. They tell me things before they happen."

The twins giggled.

"You're pulling our tails!" said Tansy.

"You're just scared," said Teasel.

"We DARE you!" they said together.

"Come on," said Bramble. "Don't be spoilsports."

"Okay," said Berry. "It'll be fun."

"All right," said Fern. "I don't want to be left behind. Wisher?"

Wisher glanced back and saw Mellow talking to Elderparr and Eldermarr, Lop and Lilly. Then she made up her mind.

"As long as we stay where Marr can see us," she said, "I'll come!"

Bramble stood on the edge of the riverbank and stared across the river. Crossing it didn't look quite so easy now. There were five stepping-stones to the

island, each one
a good leap
apart, with
fast-flowing
water in
between.

"Oh, dear,"
he said. "I wish I
hadn't said I'd go first!"

But there was no turning back.
The others were lining up behind him.

"Hurry up," said Tansy.

"We're waiting," said Teasel.

"Here goes!" said Bramble. He leapt
from the bank on to the first stone. It was
very slippery and he wobbled.

"Well done!" shouted Bracken.

"Be careful!" said Fern.

"I'm okay," shouted Bramble.
"Nothing to it."

Which wasn't true. He thought the next rock looked further away. I hope I make it, he thought. Bramble steadied himself – then sprang!

"Hooray!" cheered Bracken, Berry, Fern, Wisher, Tansy and Teasel.

When Bramble had made it to the fourth rocky step, Bracken followed. He was trembling so much he nearly slipped off the bank. But he jumped on to the first stone, then sat there – plucking up courage to go on.

"I'll go next," said Tansy. "I think Bracken needs some help."

One by one, the rabbits made the crossing to River Island. After Tansy came Fern, then Wisher, followed by Berry. Last came Teasel.

"Phew!" he said, jumping safely off the fifth stone on to River Island. "I'm glad I didn't fall in. I was afraid the pike would get me!"

"Pike?" said Bramble, Bracken, Berry, Fern and Wisher.

"Er, yes," said Tansy. "Didn't we mention him? He's a big, scary fish!"

Teasel pointed to a clump of reeds, near the bank where the water was calm.

"The mean old pike lives there,"
he said.

"He's got sharp teeth," said Tansy.
"He eats anything!"

"Wriggly worms!" said Bramble.

"Slugs and snails," said Bracken.

"Creeping caterpillars!" said Berry.

"Bugs and beetles," said Fern.

Wisher's ears tingled for what felt like
the hundredth time that day. She had
a bad feeling about the pike.

Tansy and Teasel looked admiringly
at them all.

"You were brilliant!" said Tansy. "I
was scared too."

Bramble, Bracken, Berry, Fern and
Wisher felt proud. It was the most daring
thing they'd ever done in their lives!

Ducklings
in
Danger!
5

River Island was small enough for the
rabbits to stand in the middle and see all
around it. Bramble, Bracken, Bramble,
Fern and Wisher had never been on an
island before. They were amazed – and
just a little bit alarmed – to be completely
surrounded by water. The sound of the
river tumbling over the waterfall was
so noisy they had to shout to make
themselves heard.

"See that?" cried Tansy, pointing to an old tree at the far end of the island. "It's our most secret *secret* place. Race you there!"

It took Bracken exactly twenty-two leaps and a hop to reach the tree. He arrived first.

"Wow!" said Teasel, coming second. "You run fast!"

Tansy and Teasel took Bramble, Bracken, Berry, Fern and Wisher inside the hollow trunk of the tree. There wasn't much room, but no one minded. Tansy held up a toadstool, wrinkly with age, and said, "We must all promise on this toadstool never to tell anyone about our secret place."

Berry got the giggles and Tansy gave him a look.

"We'd better do as she says," whispered Teasel. "She gets cross if we don't do this properly!"

The seven rabbits put their paws on the toadstool and made the vow. Suddenly Wisher stood up. Now the tips of her ears were tingling more than ever.

"There's trouble!" she said. "I know it!"

The rabbits scrambled out of the tree trunk. They heard the sound of noisy quacking.

Quack, quack, quack!

"It's Daisy Duck!" cried Wisher. "Her ducklings are in danger!"

The rabbits watched as Daisy and her ducklings were swept downriver. Soon they would be over the waterfall. The tiny ducklings spun round and round, helpless against the force of the water.

"I wish there was something we could do," said Wisher.

Quack, *quack, quack!*

Mellow, Eyebright, Willow, Lop and Lilly
heard the commotion. They rushed to the
riverbank.

"It's Daisy Duck!" said Mellow.

Daisy's ducklings were in the middle
of the river, paddling furiously against the
strong current. Daisy was trying to push
them towards the bank, to calmer water.
But Mellow saw the little birds were
heading for a rocky waterfall – fast!

"Help!" cried Daisy. "Please help!"

"What can we do?" said Lilly.

"We must think of something," said
Lop.

Eyebright and Willow watched
anxiously.

"Poor little things!" they said.

Mellow's head was in a spin. Then she
had an idea.

"I know, we'll make a chain across the stepping-stones," she said. "We'll try to stop them with in our paws."

"But the ducklings are so small," said Willow. "They'll slip through."

"Oh, no! You're right!" said Mellow. "We need something to make a barrier."

Eyebright pointed to a fallen branch floating in the water.

"Will that do?" he said.

"It's big," said Mellow. "But it might work. Let's pull it together. We must block their way!"

Mellow went first across the stepping-stones, and Eyebright, Willow, Lop and Lilly came behind her. It was difficult for the rabbits to keep their balance because they were pulling the branch through the water. They wobbled so much on the slippery rocks Mellow was sure they'd all fall in! But, at last, they held the barrier in place across the river.

Daisy quacked frantically. She hoped Mellow's plan to save her ducklings would work.

"Wait by the bank!" called Mellow. "We'll push them your way. Ready? Here they come!"

They counted the ducklings as they swirled, then bumped into the twiggy barrier.

"One . . .

two . . .

three . . .

four . . .

five . . ."

The sixth, smallest duckling, slipped through. They had rescued all of Daisy's ducklings – except one.

"OH NO!" cried Bramble, Bracken, Berry, Fern, Wisher, Tansy and Teasel, watching from River Island. They saw the duckling disappear.

Mellow caught sight of them first, and leapt from her stepping-stone to join them.

"Stars above!" she cried. "How did you get here?"

She was followed by Eyebright, Willow, Lop and Lilly.

"Tansy! Teasel!" cried Lilly. "You wait till I get you home!"

"Time for explanations later," said Mellow, looking hard at Bramble, Bracken, Berry, Fern and Wisher.

"Did anyone see where the duckling went?"

Wisher was trying to concentrate. A voice whispered inside her head, but she couldn't hear the words. Everyone was talking at once and the sound of the waterfall was deafening.

Wisher moved away to a quieter place to listen. She stopped by a bed of reeds and heard a voice say:

I whisper a song like the wind in your ear.
Wisher, look down. Wisher, look here!

Daisy Duck left her five ducklings safely on the riverbank, then swam over to the island. She was quacking louder than ever.

Quack, *quack,* *quack!*

"P-p-p-p-pike!" she cried.

The young rabbits knew what Daisy meant at once.

"The pike!" they shouted.

"Pike?" said Mellow. "Is that mean old fish still around?"

"I'm afraid so," said Eldermarr Willow.

"No wonder poor Daisy is frantic," said Elderparr Eyebright.

"Tansy told us the pike eats ANYTHING!" said Fern. "Ooo! If he sees the duckling . . ."

"Yes, yes," said Mellow quickly. "I think Daisy knows what might happen, Fern."

"We know where the pike lives," said Tansy.

"In the reeds," said Teasel. "Over there."

"Run!" said Mellow. "Oh, I hope we're not too late!"

Everyone raced after Tansy and Teasel. To their astonishment, Wisher was already there.

"I heard a voice," she said. "It told me to look for the duckling here."

They all peered into a thick clump of reeds growing at the water's edge.

The reeds grew closely together
and made it difficult to see between
the stalks. Then they heard the
faintest noise. And THERE
was the little duckling,
trapped in the stems.

What Wisher saw next
made her gasp. A flash of
silver below the surface of
the water. The flick of a tail.
The glint of an eye. A long, dark shape
shot from the reeds and made straight for
the stranded duckling!

"Marr!" shouted Wisher.

"Where?" cried Mellow.

Quack, quack, quack! cried Daisy.

All the rabbits jumped into the shallow water and splashed about. The commotion gave the old pike the fright of his life! With a snap of his jaws, he took off as fast as he could go.

Daisy rushed to rescue and comfort her frightened little duckling.

"Thank you," she said, smiling at everyone. "You've helped to save ALL my precious babies!"

Then Mellow and the others watched
Daisy carry her last little duckling on her
back across the river. Everyone cheered to
see the six ducklings happily reunited.

Quack! Quack! Quack!

The Great Rabbit Rescue
6

"You were very naughty!" said Mellow, as she sat surrounded by Bramble, Bracken, Berry, Fern and Wisher. "It was dangerous coming to the island."

"What were you thinking?" said Lilly to Tansy and Teasel.

"We're sorry!" said the young rabbits.

"But if the children hadn't been here," said Eldermarr Willow, "Wisher may not have found Daisy's duckling."

"That's true,"
said Mellow.

"Our problem now,"
said Elderparr Eyebright, "is getting
everyone safely *off* the island."

"They can't go back across the
stepping-stones," said Lilly. "The water is
deeper now. It's nearly covered the rocks."

"And the current is too strong," said
Lop. "They'll be swept away."

"When we came, I nearly fell in,"
said Berry.

"Me too," said Bracken.

"Will we have to stay here for EVER?"
said Fern.

"No," said Mellow. "I'm sure we'll find a way. Let's *think*."

While the parents and elders were thinking, Tansy and Teasel played Hop-Back, and the young Longears joined in. Watching them gave Mellow an idea.

"Hop-back!" she said. "That's it! The children can hop across our backs!"

"Brilliant!" said Lop.

"It's risky," said Lilly.

"It might work," said Willow.

"Let's give it a try!" said Eyebright.

"Right," said Mellow. "There's no time to lose!"

Mellow, Lop and Lilly, Eyebright and Willow stood side by side along the five stepping-stones —each was about one rabbit-leap apart. Then they bent over.

"Ready?" Mellow called to the children. "Now hop across on our backs!"

The young rabbits lined up, excited, and just a little nervous.

"I'll go first," said Berry. "You can watch me fall in!"

"Don't!" said Fern. "You're making me scared."

"You'll be okay," said Tansy.

"Here goes!" said Berry.

Bramble, Bracken, Fern, Wisher, Tansy and Teasel watched him leap from the island on to Mellow's back.

He looked round and grinned.

"Go on," said Bramble.

"Okay, okay," said Berry. "Don't rush me."

He crouched, wriggled, then sprang from Mellow on to Elderparr Eyebright's back. A leap took him to Eldermarr Willow, who nearly overbalanced. A big hop brought him to Lilly . . . and another leap to Lop. Berry jumped off Lop on to the riverbank.

"I did it!" he cried, and flipped a somersault.

"Well done!" said Mellow. "You next, Bramble."

After him came Bracken, then Fern, Wisher, Tansy and Teasel. Over they went to the other side. When at last Mellow, Lop and Lilly, Eyebright and Willow leapt on to the bank, they were greeted by cheers

from a great many rabbits. Everyone
living at Burrow Bank had turned out to
watch the Great Rabbit Rescue!

Daisy Duck was there too, quacking
noisily. She waddled off home with her
ducklings. She couldn't wait to spread the
good news!

The story spread like wildfire along the
riverbank.

"Have you heard?" said Daisy when
she met Sylvia Squirrel. "So much has
happened today. I don't know where to
begin.

Terrible! One thing after another. My ducklings were nearly lost for ever! One went missing, you see? Nearly eaten by a pike! The biggest fish you've ever seen. Rabbits too. Twelve or more! Stuck on an island. Mellow was marvellous. Came to the rescue. What a rabbit!"

"Goodness!" said Sylvia. And she hurried off to tell someone. The first friend she saw was Violet Vole.

"Have you heard?" said Sylvia. "Daisy's ducklings were eaten by an enormous fish. Lost for ever, poor things! Mellow got stuck on an island. It took sixteen rabbits to rescue her!"

"A terrible tale!" said Violet. "I must spread the news at once. She rushed along the riverbank and the first friend she saw was Barley. He was waiting at the little wooden bridge for Mellow and the others to return.

"Have you heard?" said Violet. "Mellow was nearly eaten by a great big fish with enormous teeth! Daisy's ducklings got stuck on an island with lots of rabbits. Twenty at least! But Mellow rescued everyone. I think that's right."

"Oh, buttercups!" said Barley. "I *knew* something dreadful would happen today. Where is Mellow now? Are the children all right?"

"I don't know," said Violet. "But I'm sure they'll be back soon. I must be off. Goodbye!"

Violet left Barley pacing up and down on the bridge, tugging his whiskers with worry.

Mellow kissed her parents goodbye. It was time to leave Burrow Bank and go home. Bramble, Bracken, Berry, Fern and Wisher promised Elderparr Eyebright and Eldermarr Willow they would come again soon.

"Come and see us too," said Tansy and Teasel.

"We will!" they said.

"We haven't had such an exciting day in a long time," said Lilly.

"You must visit us," said Mellow. "Barley would love to meet you. He won't believe his ears when I tell him what we did today!"

Then she set off along the riverbank with the young rabbits. The late afternoon sun was warm on their backs as they hopped and skipped around puddles on the path. Mellow found it difficult to believe the rain had caused so much trouble. The river was now calm, flowing along in the same Not-Such-A-Hurry way as it usually did.

Whooo-Wheeep!

The peace was shattered by a piercing whistle. The Red Dragon came clattering down the track, and the rabbits stood back. He went by so fast the wind flattened their fur.

"He's in a hurry to get home!" said Mellow.

"Elderparr Eyebright says he doesn't mean any harm," said Bramble. "I'm not *quite* so scared of him any more."

Bracken, Berry and Wisher nodded. They agreed.

"Well, I am!" said Fern. "He's a great big monster!"

Mellow smiled.

"Monster or not," she said, "you must all stay away from his tracks!"

Along the way, they took a shortcut across a cornfield. The crop was high, ready for harvesting, and they stopped to nibble some corn.

They saw some mice in amongst the golden stalks, enjoying a picnic too.

While they were eating, a shadow passed overhead. Bramble was on the look-out. He thumped his foot three times to warn the others.

Thump, thump, thump!

"Burdock!" he said.

"Down," whispered Mellow.

They crouched, still as stones. Mellow looked up and saw the huge buzzard circling slowly in the sky, a short distance away. Hunting. Searching.

Then he dived!
Mellow closed her
eyes. She thought
she heard the faint
squeak of mouse.
She looked again
and saw Burdock
flying away.

"Quick!" said Mellow, when she was
sure he had gone. "Run! As fast as you
can. We're nearly home."

Barley saw them racing from the corn
field. His heart was beating so fast, he
thought it would burst. He had seen
Burdock fly up, and thought the worst.
Now he hopped up and down for joy to
see them safe.

"Oh!" he cried, as Mellow, Bramble,
Bracken, Berry, Fern and Wisher ran
across the bridge to him.

"I've heard such stories. I thought I'd
never see you all again!"

"Barley Longears!" said Mellow,
hugging him tight. "I told you I'd bring
everyone safely back. And I did!"

Later that night, when the young rabbits were snug in the burrow, Mellow and Barley sat talking.

"It's been quite a day," said Mellow. "Let me tell you all about it . . ."